If you visited a Greenland shark, you'd get very chilly!

Greenland sharks live in the icy-cold Arctic Ocean, where the water freezes over in the winter.

These sharks have special anti-freeze in their bodies, which stops them turning to ice!

You'd better not be afraid of the dark! Frilled sharks live in the inky-blackness of the deep sea.

There's not much food at the bottom of the sea, so these sharks have to eat any rotting, old or dead animals they can find...yum!

You'd have great fun swimming around colourful coral reefs with a whitetip reef shark.

The fish that live here are beautiful but this shark likes to eat them, so don't be surprised if they all scarper and hide!

Would you rather...

have a porbeagle shark for your dad,

a Port Jackson shark for your mother,

a sand tiger shark
for a sister,

or an electric ray
for a brother?

You would have fun with this dad but you might get covered in stinky seaweed!

Porbeagle sharks are big and strong and seem to like games. They throw their food about, play with bits of rubbish and even roll in seaweed – just for fun!

Come back Mum!

This shark mum wouldn't take very good care of you.

She'd lay you in an egg called a mermaid's purse – but then she'd abandon you! When Port Jackson pups hatch, they have to take care of themselves.

If you had a sand tiger shark for a sister, you would have one simple choice to make: are you going to eat her or is she going to eat you?

A sand tiger shark mum might have several shark pups, but the strongest ones eat the smaller ones while they are still inside her body!

You'd better be nice to your electric ray brother or he might zap you!

Electric rays belong to the same family as sharks but can stun or kill their fish prey with an electric shock.

Would you rather look like...

a carpet shark,

a hammerhead shark,

a lantern shark,

or a bull shark?

Watch out! You might get stepped on if you looked like a carpet shark.

These sharks have amazing camouflage. Their colours, shapes and patterns help them blend in perfectly when they rest on the seabed.

Ouch!

You'd have super eyesight if you had a head like a hammerhead shark!

A strange head helps these sharks to change direction quickly. They have nifty eyes at both ends of their wide head which might also help them find their fast-moving prey.

If you flashed like a lantern shark, you'd be able to find your way in the deep, dark sea!

Lantern sharks have flashing lights on their bodies. It might be a smart way of finding other fish to eat but no one knows for sure.

If you had skin like a bull shark, you'd be covered all over in tiny little scales!

Tiny tooth-like scales form an armour that protects bull sharks from hungry fish, but bigger sharks and killer whales can still take a bite...

Would you rather...

have a barbecue with a great white shark,

a take-away with a basking shark,

or a picnic with a
tiger shark?

You'd have to be very hungry to enjoy a barbecue with a great white shark!

This shark has a huge appetite for meat and fish. She'll eat the equivalent of about 3000 burgers before she is full up.

You'd really be eating on the go with a basking shark!

These sharks have massive mouths. As they swim, seawater flows in – along with thousands of little animals, such as shrimps and baby fish.

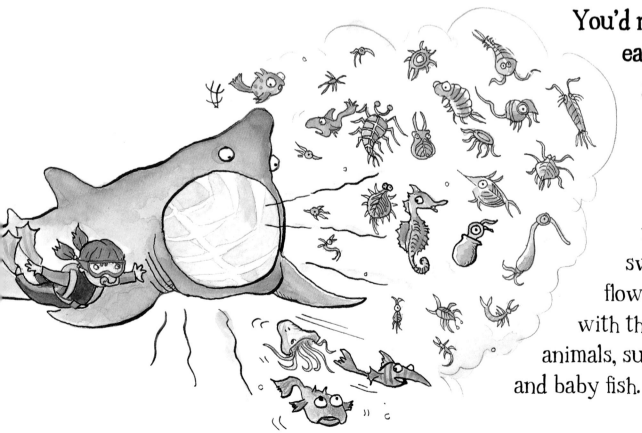

A tiger shark isn't at all fussy about food so
you'd have to eat all sorts on this picnic!

Some people call tiger sharks 'bins with fins'
because they gobble up almost anything they
find. Some tiger sharks have even been found with
metal, glass and rubber tyres in their tummies.

Would you rather have teeth like...

a lemon shark,

a leopard shark,

a longnose sawshark,

or a whale shark?

You'd have five rows of mega-sized sharp teeth!

Perfect for wrapping your jaws around a slippery, wriggling fish! A lemon shark traps fish in its rows of teeth and shakes its head from side to side, to quickly chomp and munch its prey.

You'd keep the tooth fairy busy! A leopard shark loses its teeth all the time...

Leopard sharks munch crunchy food, such as crabs, so they can lose up to 20,000 teeth in their lifetime. Luckily, they are always growing new ones!

You'd have around 40 ultra-sharp teeth on your super-sensitive snout!

A longnose sawshark uses its snout to sense other animals in the water. It's also a deadly weapon to slash and slice.

It would take ages to brush your teeth!

Whale sharks are the biggest fish in the world, but they have the tiniest teeth – around 3000 of them! No one knows why because they don't need teeth at all. They swallow their fishy meals whole.

Shark Awards!

Which shark would you rather be?

Sand tiger shark

The Smartest Shark

Humans have bigger brains than sharks (about 240 times as big) but that doesn't mean sharks are dim! Sand tiger sharks are super smart and even hunt shoals of fish together.

Hammerhead shark

The Friendliest Shark

Most sharks live alone but some female hammerheads swim together in groups of up to 500 sharks. No one knows why!

Frilled shark

The Smiliest Shark

Frilled sharks swim with their mouths open – showing off their rows of lovely white teeth. It makes them look as if they are smiling!

The Bravest Shark

The bravest shark award goes to the basking shark. These giants happily swim with people, which takes a lot of courage because humans kill millions of sharks every year.

Basking shark

Great white shark

The Deadliest Shark

Great white sharks mostly like eating seals and dolphins, but occasionally they attack humans by mistake – making them the most deadly of all sharks.

The Spottiest Shark

Leopard sharks have lovely deep brown spots on their yellow skin. This pattern helps camouflage the sharks as they rest on the seabed.

Leopard shark

More Shark Fun!

Stay safe and ask a grown-up to help you.

How big?

Use a measuring tape or ruler to find out just how big the world's longest and smallest sharks are. Whale sharks can reach 12 metres long, or even more! The world's smallest sharks are pygmy sharks and dwarf lantern sharks. These sharks are only 20–30 cm long.

Investigate!

Sharks have lots of teeth, and most of them are sharp and pointed. Use a mirror to find out how many teeth you have. Are they different sizes and shapes? How many teeth do grown-ups have?

Would you rather...?

Think of some 'Would you rather...?' questions to share with your friends or family. Visit your local library and research different sharks to create your own fun questions.

Shark aquarium

Ask an adult for a clean, empty jam jar. Paint one of your favourite sharks on thick paper and cut it out. Use sticky tape to fix the end of some wire to the shark. Then fix the other end of the wire to the inside lid of your jar. Pour some blue glitter in your jar, then screw the lid on so your shark sits inside, and turn the jar upside down.

Q Quarto Knows

Quarto is the authority on a wide range of topics.
Quarto educates, entertains and enriches the lives of our readers—enthusiasts and lovers of hands-on living.
www.quartoknows.com

Publisher: Zeta Jones
Associate Publisher: Maxime Boucknooghe
Designer: Victoria Kimonidou
Editor: Sophie Hallam
Art Director: Laura Roberts-Jensen
Editorial Director: Victoria Garrard

Copyright © QED Publishing 2016

First published in hardback in the UK in 2015 by QED Publishing,
Part of The Quarto Group, The Old Brewery, 6 Blundell Street, London, N7 9BH

A catalogue record for this book is available from the British Library.

ISBN 978 1 78493 198 8

Printed in China